CW01582819

To my beautiful daughters, partner and my entire family.

Copyright © 2019 by Tiny Angel Press LTD.

All rights reserved.

No part of this book may be reproduced, stored in a retrieval system, or transmitted in any form or by any means, electronic, mechanical, photocopying, recording, scanning, or otherwise, without the prior written permission of the publisher.

https://themonster-series.com

Illustrations by Dmitry Chizhov

Thanks to author Karen McMillan for her assistance with this project.

ISBN: 978-1-9162194-4-1

In collaboration with Duckling Publishing and Chrissy Metge Ltd.
www.ducklingpublishing.com
www.chrissymetge.com

Duckling publishing

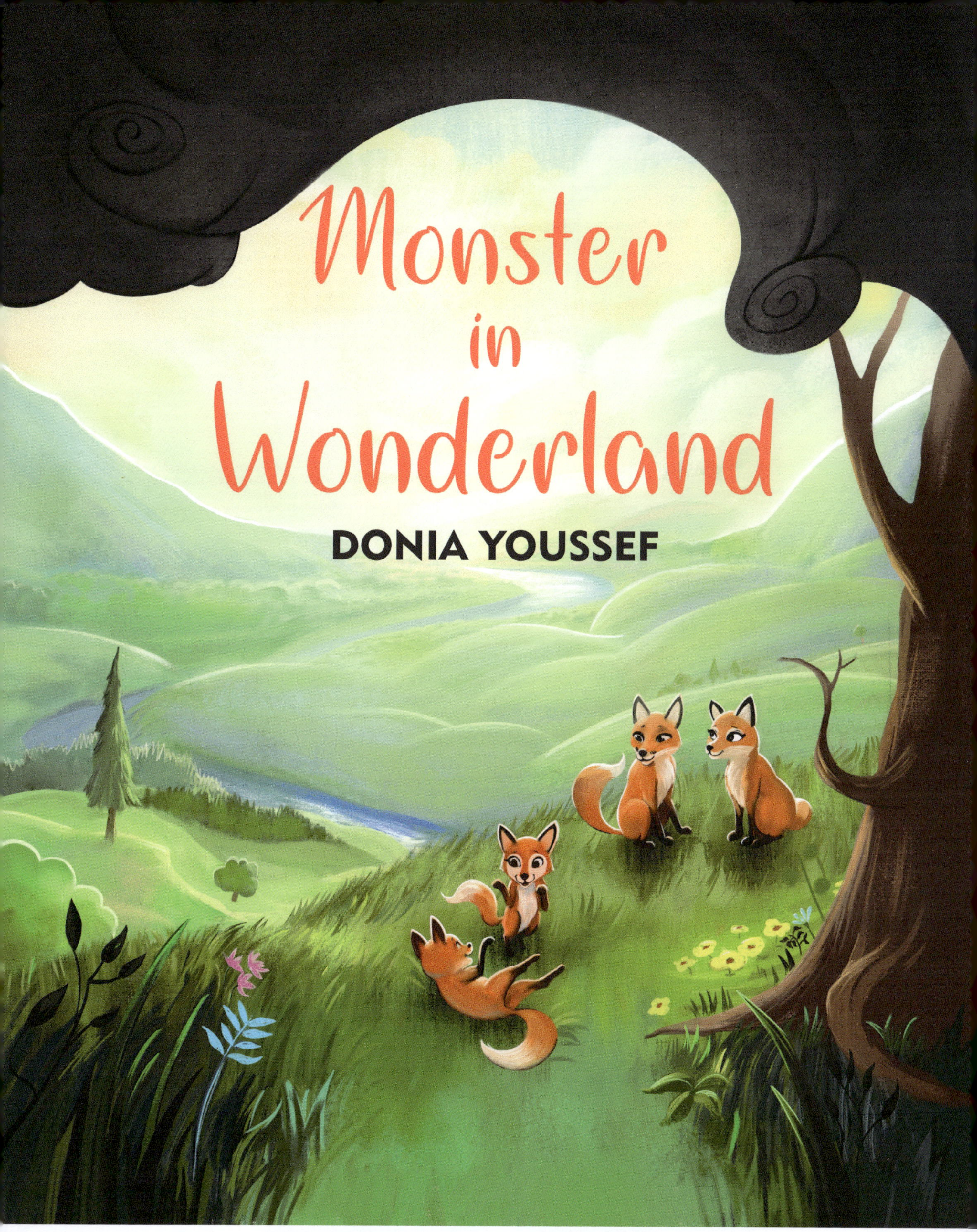
Monster
in
Wonderland
DONIA YOUSSEF

Far over the hills and through the dales, under the vast sky, and in a valley nestled between two mountains, there lived a family of foxes. They lived in a foxhole on a grassy down, and they loved each other with all their hearts.

There was a mummy, daddy, and two baby foxes. The baby foxes were named Tiana and Aaliyah.

Tiana and Aaliyah dashed out of their foxhole each morning into the bright sunshine. They leapt over dewy grass and waved their beautiful bushy tails at the birds in the trees. The birds sang a song, and the girls hurried to the river, where they drank to their hearts' content.

When they returned to their foxhole, Mummy had prepared breakfast. Everyone sat in a circle as sunlight streamed in from outside. It was springtime in the valley of Wonderland, and everyone was happy and hopeful.

After breakfast, the fox family ran outside to hunt and play. And this was their life, happy in their foxhole, in the valley, in Wonderland where the grass was green, and the sun shone like gold.

But one day, the sky, once blue and bright, began to darken.

'What's happening, Mummy?' Tiana asked.

Mummy sniffed the air and frowned. 'Get inside, girls,' she said. 'Hurry on now.'

Tiana and Aaliyah listened to Mummy and hurried inside their foxhole. Daddy ran out and said, 'What is it?'

Mummy shook her head. 'I sense danger.'

And Mummy Fox was right, for the very next moment, lightning struck nearby. Animals fled to their homes as rain poured from the heavens.

Daddy and Mummy began to run back to their foxhole as the sky cracked and the dark clouds moved over.

Daddy ran inside but then turned and discovered that Mummy was not by his side.

'Mummy?' wailed Tiana and Aaliyah. 'Where are you?'

Mummy stood on top of the grassy down under a tall oak tree as lightning flashed and thunder cracked.

There, surrounded by dim light, was a shadowy monster. Not any monster, but a monster that had come for her. The monster was big and had no face. The shadowy monster crept up close.

‘I am not afraid,’ Mummy Fox said.

She was a brave fox, and she would protect her family from the monster. But the monster moved over her and suddenly she was sick.

Daddy ran outside, along with Tiana and Aaliyah, and they helped Mummy back inside the foxhole.

Mummy felt sick. Daddy and the girls prepared a bed of straw and they laid her down. Tiana brought water, and Aaliyah brought a small pillow made of feathers.

'It was a monster!' said Tiana. 'I saw it outside. It cast a spell over Mummy.'

Aaliyah shivered. 'How can we help?'

Mummy said, 'We have to travel through Wonderland to the Enchanted Forest. There, the Wise Owl lives in his oak tree, and he will tell us what to do to break the monster's spell.'

The next morning, Daddy and the girls were ready to go to the Enchanted Forest when Mummy came outside. 'I'm going with you,' she said.

'But you're sick,' Daddy Fox said. 'You need to rest.'

'Look around,' Mummy said. 'Our grassy down is covered in fog, and a monster haunts the land. You'll need my help.'

Daddy knew Mummy was right, but he was afraid, for she could barely stand. 'You're sure you'll be okay?'

'We'll help, Mummy,' the girls said. The two baby foxes pushed their tiny fox heads up under Mummy's armpits. 'Is that better?' they asked.

Mummy nodded. 'Thank you.'

Together, the fox family travelled through the darkness of Wonderland. The monster had covered the land in fog and a shroud of night. The sun didn't shine, and the only way forward was by dim moonlight.

Suddenly, there was a loud noise. It sounded like a whistle.

The fox family turned to see a monster with silver ears and a bright shiny nose. Smoke rose from its head and blew out of its mouth. Each time the smoke blew out, it whistled loudly.

'A machine!' Daddy cried.

'Hurry!' Tiana said, motioning her tail toward the Enchanted Forest.

The fox family darted through the dry yellow grass, and the family entered the safety of the Enchanted Forest.

Little glints of light sparkled here and there inside the Enchanted Forest, thanks to the fairies and forest sprites. But even here, something was wrong.

The fox family began to cough.

'Smoke,' Mummy said. 'The machine monster has brought it's pollution here, too.'

Fauns and stags lay near a stream, too tired to move.

Birds, big and small, hawks and sparrows and robins, were in their nests, too sick to fly.

Little bugs and worms rested underground, for they were too sick to carry.

‘The monster’s dark spell has come here, too,’ Mummy said. She coughed.

‘You need to rest,’ Daddy said.

The fox family lay near the stream by the fauns and stags. Other foxes were nearby, too.

'What has happened?' said a baby fox, a stranger to the fox family.

'A monster came,' Tiana and Aaliyah Fox said. 'It cast a dark spell on our mummy and now it is in the Enchanted Forest, too.'

The baby fox shook her head and hurried back to her family.

'Where is the Wise Owl?' Daddy asked. 'We must find him soon.'

'There!' said Tiana. 'We can ask the fairies.'

Tiana and Aaliyah darted through the smoky woods until they came upon a trio of tiny fairies who fluttered in the air near a large rock that glowed with a golden light.

'Can you tell us where the Wise Owl lives?' Tiana asked.

The fairies began to hum, and it was the most beautiful music Tiana and Aaliyah had ever heard.

Then the fairies pointed their small magic wands to the west.

'There!' the fairies exclaimed.

The girls ran back to their parents and told them the direction the fairies had pointed out.

'Tomorrow we go,' Mummy said.

The next day, they travelled west through the Enchanted Forest until the fox family came to a crossroads. They didn't know which way to go.

Something grumbled and the foxes turned. A tall old tree, with a face, smiled warmly.

'They call me Arbol,' said the old tree. 'And I imagine you, fox family, are lost. Am I right?'

The foxes nodded. 'A monster has cast a spell on me,' said Mummy Fox. 'We seek the Wise Owl.'

'Oh, yes,' said the old tree Arbol. 'He's deeper inside the forest. Take the road on your right'.

The foxes thanked Arbol and hurried down the road to their right. But they couldn't go very far into the thickest part of the Enchanted Forest because Mummy was too weak.

'The monster's spell is getting worse,' Tiana said.

Daddy and the girls helped Mummy walk, but she was weaker.

'Look,' Mummy said. 'I see the Wise Owl.'

And there, in the heart of the Enchanted Forest, everyone turned to see an oak tree with an owl sitting in it.

'Wise Owl!' Aaliyah shouted. 'Is it you?'

The owl had brown and silver feathers. It lifted its chin and looked down with its big eyes that looked like yellow moons.

'Ah,' the Wise Owl said in a deep voice. 'You've made it. I've been expecting you, fox family.'

The Wise Owl told the fox family that he, too, had been sick, but animals from all over the forest had brought him fruit and vegetables.

'You must find the villagers who will help you,' said the Wise Owl. 'You, Mummy Fox, must be brave and find a red-haired girl named Joy. Darkness might rule the land right now, but with your help, we'll defeat it!'

The fox family walked in the direction that the Wise Owl pointed, but to do so, they had to go in the direction where the metal machine was still huffing and puffing. They walked again through dry yellow grass, but the machine was too quick. Tiana fell and was about to be swallowed up by the metal machine when suddenly a little girl with red hair snatched the baby fox up in her arms.

'You'll be all right!' the little red-haired girl said. 'Come with me.'

'She must be the girl the Wise Owl spoke of,' said Mummy Fox.

The little red-haired girl carried Tiana along a winding path, and the fox family followed.

Soon, they came upon an entrance to some woods.

'Here you go, little fox,' said the red-haired girl. 'I hope you're okay. My name's Joy. That machine now goes straight through our village and it has been destroyed, so we now live in this forest.'

'Thank you,' Tiana said, but it came out as a little bark, for she couldn't speak the human's language.

'Come with me, little ones,' said Joy. 'We'll find people who will help you.'

As they walked further, they discovered a section of the forest untouched by darkness, and amazingly, there were roses of all colours. And there, standing next to the roses, were smiling villagers, holding baskets of fruit and vegetables. There were baskets of bananas, broccoli, oranges, cabbages, carrots, cherries and tomatoes and much more.

Mummy smiled. ‘These will give me the strength to fight the monster’s spell.’

‘Go on, girls,’ said Daddy. ‘Gather the fruits and vegetables for Mummy.’

One of the men holding a basket of bananas smiled at the two little foxes as they came to gather the fruits and vegetables. He gave the girls two small baskets, and they quickly filled them. The two foxes thanked the man. Carrying the baskets in their mouths they hurried off to save Mummy.

Soon, after eating the fruits and vegetables, Mummy had the strength to carry on.

‘We must find the Wise Owl again,’ said Daddy. ‘We must thank him, but I don’t know how to retrace our steps.’

‘I think I know where you might find him,’ said Joy. She pointed toward the heart of the Enchanted Forest. ‘I saw him over there just a moment ago.’

Tiana and Aaliyah rubbed up against Joy’s legs, and Joy bent down and petted their furry heads. They walked a little way and it wasn’t long before they were thanking the Wise Old for his help.

Mummy Fox suddenly felt warm, and a bright, brilliant light shone on her from above.

The dark spell, the monster's spell, flew out of her. The mysterious shadowy monster disappeared out of sight.

Mummy stood up straight. 'I feel well again,' she said. 'Thank you, Wise Owl.'

And together, along with the Wise Owl and all the animals, fairies, and creatures of the Enchanted Forest, they rid the land of darkness. They spread the good news of the fruit and vegetables, of love, of family, and of being brave during the darkest of times.

The shadowy monster and its machine had no chance.

The shadowy monster growled and howled and whistled and whined from far off in the distance, but the monster and his machine moved away, knowing the good animals and people of Wonderland had defeated them.

The fairies in the Enchanted Forest directed everyone to the villagers and their food, and soon everyone was healthy again.

Later, Joy and her family returned and rebuilt their village.

And the fox family lived happily ever after, back in their foxhole, in the grassy down, under the wide blue skies of the joyful valley of Wonderland.

The End.

Each book helps to tell the story of surviving cancer. I wrote the first book because while I was going through my own treatment, I found very little literature on how to explain what was happening to my two young daughters.

After I released my first book *The Monster in Mummy*, I became more and more involved with different charities and organisations. Other cancer survivors then started to contact me and telling me their own stories. I realised there is so much we as a society are not aware of especially when it comes to what cancer survivors go through. Their stories are so powerful and yet we hardly heard from patients. Why is that? I am so humble and proud to be able to bring you these stories and help raise awareness that behind every cancer diagnostic is a real person.

Donia Youssef, Author & Producer of *The Monster series*.

Printed in Great Britain
by Amazon

49475289R00023